Adopted By Wolves

Dream Big!

Stephanie Poole

Adopted By Wolves

Written and Illustrated By

Stephanie Poole (age 11)

To order additional copies of this book, contact:
Xlibris Corporation
1-888-795-4274
www.Xlibris.com
Orders@Xlibris.com
59070

Contents

Table of Illustrations

Dedicated To

My Great Uncle Emmett and Great Grandmother Victoria,
who passed away recently.

To my supportive family and friends.

And to the wolves . . .

Chapter One ~ Prologue

Lost

The wind blew lightly, the forest silent. Deep in, the sound of the running paws of a wolf was the only thing to hear.

Or at least it seemed that way to Accalia and Tikaani. They hang limp in the mouth of their mother, a beautiful white wolf with black and brown markings. Accalia was a white wolf, and Tikaani was a grey wolf with a light grey underbelly. They were slipping out of their mother's mouth. Suddenly, they land with a loud thud. Their mother, Kiyiya, had thrown them into a hollow tree. She was running from something, something of which the pups did not know. Accalia yelped and howled, but her mother did not return. Tikaani opened his eyes wide, trying to see through in darkness of the tree. He jumped up, peeking out of the hole in the tree, but saw nothing. They waited minutes, hours, but Kiyiya didn't return. Something was wrong . . . she had never left her pups for this long.

The pups grew hungry, and fearful. They struggled, but managed to get out of the tree. They tumbled down, still a bit clumsy, being only one and a half month old. The air grew cold, and the skies darkened. It was late in the evening, and it would soon be dark. Accalia and Tikaani didn't know where to go. Mother had always provided for them, and the hole in the hollow tree was too high for the weak pups to climb back into. The sun began to set.

"Do you think Mother will be back soon, Tikaani?" Accalia asked with a whine.

"I don't know." He replied sadly.

They spent the long night curled up together underneath the tree. It was a cold, long, lonely, vulnerable night for the pups, but still, they slept. Sooner than the pups realized, it was morning. The skies were blue, there was dew on the trees, and all seemed peaceful. However, things were far from fine for the pups. They were alone, and far from being able to hunt for themselves. Suddenly, they heard hoof beats coming closer, and closer. Then, a herd of elk ran through the thick woods next to them. To them, it was simply amazing! They had never seen elk before! Chasing the herd was a single wolf.

"Hey! Over here!" They called, but no reply.

She didn't even stop. From what they saw, she was a tan-ish blonde she-wolf, with several different shades of colors. They could tell she was an expert hunter, with perfect focus on the elk. Desperate, they yelped, trying to call the wolf. But no answer was heard. They watched as the stranger wolf chased the elk away, until she was out of sight. They sat around the hollow tree for an hour, digging in the ground, looking for food. A mere ten feet away, was a five-foot, very steep small cliff.

Suddenly, as if simply appearing from nowhere, a majestic white she-wolf stood on the small cliff. She was Tamaska, dominant female of the Windrush Pack. Next to her, stood a pitch-black male wolf with a grey muzzle and underbelly, he was Convel, the dominant male. Accalia and Tikaani looked up at the wolves in shock and amazement. Behind the leaders, were a few members of the large pack. Suddenly, a howl from the distance, from the hunter they saw earlier. The pack answered in excited howls. None of the pack seemed to notice the pups. They were overlooked.

"I smell cubs, Tamaska, cubs that aren't ours, which means an intruder!" Convel growled.

Tamaska laughed, "I have already smelled them, darling. The scent of their mother is old, which means she isn't nearby." She replied, relaxed.

Cuan, a brown wolf with a grey underbelly, a fluffy tail, and hair hanging over his eyes, barked.

"Down there!" he said, looking at Accalia and Tikaani.

The entire pack shot their eyes down at the pups. Convel slid down the steep hill and pounced on top of the pups. They yelped, and lay down on their backs in submission.

"Who are you? And where do you come from?" Convel growled, sniffing the pups.

"Relax, Convel! They are just pups!" Tamaska barked. "And besides, their mother's scent smells of a loner, not of the Midnight Howlers pack." she added.

Tamaska slid down the hill, sniffed the pups, and picked Accalia up in her jaws.

"Take her brother." Tamaska told Convel, muffled.

He did, and they walked back to their cave. It seemed like hours to the pups. They closed their eyes tightly most of the time, afraid of the pack. Suddenly, they were dropped. They opened their eyes to see a beautiful area with a pleasant cave. Inside, was a pup sitter and four pups. Three of them stared at the newcomers with different looks of confusion. The fourth could care less, she was a bit skinnier than the others, but still appeared healthy. The pack leaders walked away without another word, they were busy being leaders of such a huge pack. Cuan, the main pup-sitter, urged the pups toward each other. The brown pup walked toward Accalia

"Hi, I'm Brownie!" He said, wagging his tail

"I'm Accalia," She replied, and they became instant friends.

The white wolf pup with blondish tan face markings shrugged.

"Great. More orphans," She said rudely.

"Just leave us alone!" said Brownie. "Let me introduce, the snobby little white one is Maheegan, the black one is her brother, Caro, that one in the corner is Ginny, and, as you know, I am Brownie." he said. "And you are?" He asked.

"I am Tikaani, Accalia's brother." Tikaani replied.

Suddenly, howls and barks of joy came from the adults. The pack made way for the hunter, and a few wolves ran up to help drag the carcass.

"Nuntis is here, Nuntis is here! And she has food!" said Fluff, one of the pack members.

There, dragging the carcass was Nuntis, the beautiful blonde wolf they had seen hunting earlier.

"Easy catch! It was limping and weak." Nuntis said. The pack ate hungrily, and Cuan managed a small scrap to share with the pups. The pups ate their share, and the pack relaxed for the evening. Accalia made good friends with Brownie, and they talked most of the day.

"Is Tamaska your mother?" Accalia asked curiously.

"No. My mother was a delta that got pregnant and was kicked out. Luckily, they didn't throw me out with her. It would be safer with the pack." Brownie replied.

Meanwhile, Tikaani tried to make friends with Ginny. He inched toward her, closer and closer. He stopped a foot from her.

"Hi, I'm Tikaani," he said softly.

She looked at him, unsure.

"Yeah . . . hi," she said in a rather bored voice.

It was clear she was in no mood for mingling, and Tikaani walked away. When night came, the pups all curled up together . . . except for Ginny. She huddled up in the corner of the den, and slept. Accalia felt comfortable with her apparent new pack, but she couldn't sleep well. She dozed in and out, and finally slept. She awoke the next morning happily, the sun shined through the trees, the slightly cool breeze blew her fur gently, and she felt at home. Little did she know there was a stranger lurking behind her, ready to pounce.

Chapter Two

Danger

Just then, Accalia realized that Nuntis was awake. Accalia padded over to her, looking up at the mighty huntress, who provided for the pack. She was amazed. "Morning!" Accalia said with a smile on her face. Nuntis just nodded her head and walked away. Unknown to her, toward the stranger in the forest. She sniffed the air, smelled him, and growled. Suddenly, the stranger wolf jumped out of the forest, and they began circling and snarling. The commotion woke the pack up.

"Fang!" Nuntis snarled. "Get out of our territory, NOW!"

Fang chuckled "Morning to you too, lovely."

He hadn't noticed that the leaders were awake. Nuntis scratched his face, leaving a scratch across his eye. He grunted, but to the wolves' surprise, he didn't attack. All the pups ran into the den, watching from safety. Convel jumped upon Fang, sinking his teeth into Fang's neck. Fang scrambled, trying to get up, and Convel let go. And as fast as he arrived, he disappeared into the woods. The pups gasped and whispered to each other. Cuan, the pup sitter, ran into the den and wrapped his fluffy tail around the pups.

"Why didn't he fight back?" Accalia asked Cuan curiously.

Cuan opened his mouth to talk, but it was cut short.

"Because he is a fool." Said Nuntis, who was walking past the den. "Fang is a jerk, he acts tough, but don't let him scare you."

She finished, and walked away.

"Bloody dispersal. Can't he just find another pack to annoy?" Cuan murmured to himself.

"Hey Accalia, we saw you scramble into the den, you run so fast you could barely stop!" Maheegan laughed.

"Oh, leave her alone!" Brownie snarled, walking in between Maheegan and Accalia. "You're just jealous 'cause she is prettier than you!"

Brownie gasped quietly; he had not meant to say that aloud.

Maheegan snorted, "She wishes!" she murmured.

Cuan walked out, Accalia didn't say anything, and she seemed to blush—if a wolf could blush—a little bit.

"Thanks." She whispered to Brownie.

Just then, the large pack went out together for a hunt.

"Let us hope we catch a bull today!" Tamaska said, trying to encourage her pack.

Cuan and Fluff returned to the den after saying goodbye to the pack. Just ten minutes after the Windrush pack had left, Cuan began to pace around the entrance, while Fluff comforted the pups. The scent of an outsider grew stronger. It wasn't Fang, or a pack member. Cuan stared at the area of forest where the scent was. Suddenly, Dagger, an outsider pounced on the small Cuan. Fluff gasped, and tucked the pups into the corner of the den. She wanted to help, but she must watch the pups. As she heard Cuan gasping for breath, she made sure the pups were safe before bolting out to help her friend. She was slashed away before being pounced on by Scar, the most hardcore wolf around. He wanted to take over the pack, but was often outnumbered. As Scar grasped Fluff's neck, the pups watched in horror.

All seemed grim. They were doomed.

Fluff gasped, and went limp. Cuan struggled trying to get to his friend. Dagger didn't sink his teeth in as deep into Cuan's neck. It almost seemed as though he was just holding him hostage. Just then, Fang jumped out of the bushes, slashing deep into Scar's back, and biting the back of Dagger's neck. He swiftly jumped away, dodging a hit from them.

"Come on you big cowards!" He barked, taunting them.

Fang bolted in the forest. Scar and Dagger pursued chase. Cuan watched as they ran until they were out of sight. He ran over to Fluff.

"Fluff? FLUFF?!" He nudged his friend repeatedly trying to wake her.

She remained limp. Nuntis arrived, running so fast she could barely stop. "I left the hunt when I saw Fang running just out of our territory—he said that you all were in trouble! What happened?" Cuan looked up at her in horrified eyes . . .

Fluff wouldn't wake up. The pups began to yelp and walk out of the den. Nuntis ran in and blocked the view. *'The pups shouldn't see this.'* she thought.

Convel and Tamaska arrived in a few minutes, with the pack behind them.

"Nuntis! Why did you go-" She stopped, looking at Fluff's body laying there. She sniffed the air, and smelled the outsiders, including Fang.

"Fang helped us." Cuan told the alphas "He actually protected us . . . he probably—dare I say it—saved my life, mine and the pups."

The alphas seemed shocked "Scar and Dagger . . . they did this, didn't they?" Convel said after sniffing the air.

Cuan nodded, and Convel let out a snarl more like a roar. "They will pay for this . . . what they did to poor Fluff."

Just then, Fluff groaned, and she breathed weakly. Cuan jumped up

"Whoa!" he yelled, shocked of his friend seemingly 'coming back from the dead.'

Nuntis stood up, and looked down at Fluff, her jaw open. Fluff was alive! As the day grew to a close, the pack settled in. They hadn't made a kill, but they could care less now. Everyone was alive . . . or so it seemed. The pack wondered what happened to Fang, who had helped them. Nuntis seemed to think about Fang the most. The pups fell asleep first, tired from such a long day. After such a dangerous day, the alphas couldn't help but wonder what tomorrow would bring.

The next morning, the alpha pair was first to get up, followed by the betas and deltas. Nuntis seemed anxious, pacing a lot, watching the forest, and the bush where Fang jumped out.

"I'm going to patrol the territory," Nuntis said.

The alpha pair nodded, and she ran into the forest.

'Come on, I have to catch their scent!' She thought. "Yes!" She said aloud.

She caught the scent! Nuntis stopped dead in her tracks. She saw what she dreaded. Scar and Dagger were on top of Fang, biting him hard. Nuntis, without hesitation, jumped in, attacking Scar and Dagger viciously. She sunk her teeth deep into Scar's back, and she left Dagger with a large gash across his hide. Nuntis had a good hold of Scar, but Dagger attacked her. Fang jumped up and jumped on Dagger, pinning him. Scar bolted away, Fang let Dagger go, and he quickly ran behind Scar. Surprisingly, Nuntis and Fang weren't too badly hurt. Fang smiled curiously at her.

"What?" She asked.

"Oh nothing . . . I owe you one," he said.

Fang began to walk away. "Aren't you going to try to join our pack?" she asked.

"No. I'm a loner." he turned around, winked at her, and ran off.

She turned and headed toward the den site, and she couldn't help but smile. As she arrived, she told the pack what happened.

She went in the den and rested with the pups. She wasn't the type to get cozy with others, and this was the first time she willingly spent time with the pups. Cuan walked in. He raised an eye and smirked at her. Tikaani and Accalia stared up at them. Cuan whispered something to her.

"I do not!" She said standing up, snarling.

Cuan lowered his head, and walked out, murmuring something to himself. Nuntis thudded down, lying down again with the pups. She sighed heavy and rested. It would probably be a while until Scar and his partner in crime, Dagger, would come back in the Windrush territory.

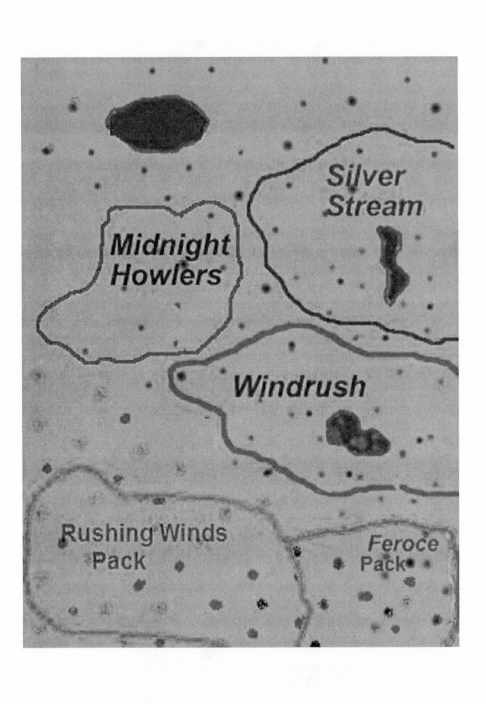

Chapter Three

Bittersweet

Two months later . . .

Two months had passed, it was winter, and without trouble. No Scar and Dagger, and hunting was good. But, it seemed like a bitter-sweet victory. There was no sign of Fang. Nuntis was patrolling the territory a lot, and never found him. She walked out into the burnt forest, out of her territory. A very risky move. However, it seemed safe. She relaxed. She couldn't help but think about it . . . *If Scar and Dagger ever found Fang* . . . she shuddered at the thought. Though Nuntis rarely showed any signs of getting close to anybody, and often ignored pups, she seemed to become a bit fond of Accalia. *I will teach her how to hunt soon.* She thought. *In a matter of days, it will be time for the pups to witness their first hunt. Accalia has the smarts to become a great huntress.* Just then, the enemy pack, the Midnight Howlers, lead by Nuntis' sister, Midnight, charged towards her. She was in their territory! She knew in her heart that she couldn't outrun them. But they would find her if she tried hiding. She tried to run, but they soon beared down upon her. They held her down biting her hard. Midnight pinned her, and sunk her teeth into Nuntis' neck until she went unconscious. They left her, kicking sand on her as they ran away. A few minutes later, a mysterious grey male tried to drag her, but couldn't, as she was too heavy. The stranger lay next to her. She couldn't stand it! She was somewhat aware of her surroundings, but couldn't do anything. She groaned. The male's cold breath on her neck sent shivers up her spine. She groaned and looked up at the male. Her vision was too blurry to see him, and she didn't feel like trying to identify him by scent. *It won't matter who he is if he is going to kill me*, Nuntis thought. Her vision came back to her, and she soon made him out. It was Fang! She stood up wobbly, and looked down at him. He smirked.

"I was attacked by the Midnight Howlers." Nuntis said.

"I know." said Fang. "But you look awfully pretty unconscious." He said with a smile.

"Look here, I'm not looking to flirt. I'm dedicated to my pack." She replied, and began to limp away.

He bounced in front of her, and play bowed.

"Could've fooled me." Fang said, chuckling.

"What makes you think that?" She said.

"Well you must have been day-dreaming about me an awful lot to not pay attention to the fact you were in their territory." Fang replied.

Nuntis couldn't help it, she laughed. She regained her strength, and went back to her pack. She told them her encounter, but failed to mention Fang. *He smells different; they won't know his scent from the enemy pack.* She thought. She went into the den, and lovingly licked the pups. Cuan and Fluff walked in. Fluff stared at her. Cuan walked over to her and sat next to her.

"Think we are fools? We know who you saw." Cuan said.

Nuntis stared at them. Her cover was blown, what would she tell them?

"What?" She said.

"You saw Fang, didn't you?" Fluff asked.

"Why would you think that? I don't smell of Fang at all!" Nuntis scoffed.

Cuan and Fluff looked at each other, and warily walked out. Nuntis sighed. The pups curled up near her fluffy tail and slept. Little did they know, tomorrow they would witness their first hunt.

Accalia woke up in a completely different surrounding. "Where am I?" She said aloud. There was sand beneath her paws, and a huge 'lake' that seemed to never end. She went over and lapped up some water, but spit it out as it had a horrible taste. Still, it seemed peaceful. She lay down, relaxing in the sun. Just then, Scar and Dagger appeared out of nowhere, and jumped on her. They clenched her neck until she went limp. She tossed and turned, but couldn't do anything. Accalia was horrified.

"Wake up! Accalia, wake up!" said a voice.

She gasped, and looked around. She was in the den, with Tikaani waking her up. *Only a dream . . .* she thought.

"We are going to the hunt!" Tikaani told her excitedly.

Accalia jumped up.

"Really? Sweet!" She barked happily.

The pack headed out. The pups were excited; they didn't realize the devastation that would happen that day.

Chapter Four

Trial and Error

The pups were tucked into a bush to watch the hunt from safety. They pursued chase on a weak bull. They cornered him, and the pack bit towards him from all directions. Lilly, the black omega female with golden eyes, jumped toward the bull. He kicked, and sent her flying backwards. She hit a tree hard and lay limp. Nuntis, who had a good hold of the bull's neck, let go and ran over to her mother. She stared at her friend in horror; Lilly had dents in her head and chest from the bull's kick. The pack brought down the bull, and ran over to the poor omega. Tamaska licked her sister's face. Convel let out mournful howls, and the pack joined in. Cuan ran over trying to hide the scene from the pups. But he was too late; the pups saw what had happened. Lilly, the beautiful pack omega, died.

"We shall savor this meal, for Lilly made the ultimate sacrifice for it!" Convel said aloud to the pack.

They said their last goodbyes to Lilly, and went over to eat. Accalia and Tikaani found it hard to eat, after watching the death of a pack member. Still, they ate. After eating, the pack headed to the den. All seemed pretty quiet, and most of the pack rested. Nuntis slipped away to the stream. The stream was half frozen, and Nuntis carefully stepped onto the ice, and sipped the cold water. She stepped off the ice carefully, and lay down by the stream. Fang lay next to her.

"I—saw Lilly's body . . ." He told her sadly.

Nuntis just nodded and lay her head on her paws. Fang placed his head on hers. *Oh great, Lilly's death and Fang just make my choice all the more difficult . . .* She thought.

Nuntis woke up. *Oh great . . . I fell asleep!* She thought. Fang was asleep still comforting her.

"Fang . . . I—I have to go." She said with a sigh.

"Hmm? Why?" he said tiredly.

They both stood up. "Because—I just do!" She said, and she ran off. Fang stared at the forest in confusion. He hung his head and walked off to his small territory. Nuntis jumped into another small stream, trying to wash off his scent. As the sun began to rise, she knew she had to get back home before they woke up. She kicked up the first snow of the season as she ran through the forest. She stopped and tumbled as she arrived at the den. In the den, she saw the pack sleeping. *Thank goodness . . .* she thought. Just as she went to lie down, Tamaska woke up, and growled low. Nuntis hung her head in submission. Tamaska gave Nuntis a hard bite around her neck.

"You didn't return last night—" Tamaska growled.

"Please, let me explain—" Nuntis began.

"Silence!" Tamaska snarled.

Convel stood next to his mate.

"You didn't return because you were with a dispersal! And you're planning to disperse!" Convel barked.

"I was only with Fang—" Nuntis began.

As the alphas began to talk, Nuntis spoke louder, "You owe him Cuan's and Fluff's lives, and probably the pup's lives, too!" Nuntis finished, and stepped back.

The other adults woke up.

"Go." Convel said. Nuntis tilted her head curiously. "I said go! You're lucky we don't chase you out, leave when you have the chance!" He yelled.

As Nuntis began to turn around, Tamaska nipped at her hide.

"Go!" She said, and she watched as Nuntis, her niece, ran off into the great unknown.

The pups were awake, and watched scared, as their parents had ordered Nuntis away. Accalia hid behind the other pups, and Brownie nuzzled her. Nuntis ran through the forest as fast as she could, she was an official dispersal. She couldn't help but think about her future.

Chapter Five

Change

The next morning, Nuntis awoke next to the lake. Snow covered half her body, and the lake was half frozen with thin ice. She stretched her stiff body and padded over to the lake where she drank the freezing water. *So I guess this is life as dispersal.* She thought. *All alone, surviving without the comfort of a pack.* She scanned the vast terrain of Yellowstone, and decided it was time to move on. Nuntis trotted through the forest, and began to run, as the cold air filled her lungs. She stopped and rested in a small area where there wasn't much snow. Suddenly, the birds flew out of the trees and the forest grew silent. Nuntis knew what this meant. She stood up, and got in a fighting position, ready for whatever was coming her way. Fang trotted out from the trees.

"Well, look what the wind blew in." He said.

Nuntis sighed in relief, "Fang! I'm a-"

"Dispersal?" He laughed. "I kind of figured that out when you came into my territory."

Nuntis looked around, there was a stream, a den, and it was close to the hunting grounds. A seemingly perfect area!

"Your territory? It's beautiful," she said.

Fang smirked and Nuntis lowered her head.

"Look, I'm sorry I left so quick-" She began

"Shh—relax, darling, it's' fine." He said, licking her cheek. You look hungry. Come now, there was a carcass over there."

Nuntis followed Fang towards the carcass, sighing deeply. *Maybe my future is bright after all.* She thought.

Three months later . . .

It was the end of winter, and the snow was starting to melt. The trees that were covered by mounds of snow were revealed. The pups were half a year old, and thriving. Ginny seemed to wander a bit farther from the pack, exploring nearly every morning. Accalia was so curious of the world outside of the territory. One morning, she awoke extra early and snuck out. A hare rustled the nearby grasses, and she gave chase. She chased and chased, and her legs grew tired. She stopped suddenly, thrust her nose in the air and sniffed.

"Oh no . . . Shoot!" Accalia told herself.

She had chased the rabbit outside of her pack territory! In addition, she smelled nearby strangers. She hid in the shrubs and peeked outside, and saw a pack searching the territory franticly. Accalia sniffed, and they weren't even the owners of the territory. As they grew closer, Accalia's eyes widened as she realized the danger she was in. It was the Midnight Howlers pack! Scar was now the dominant male, and Midnight as dominant female. *The worst possible pair. The meanest of the mean.* Dagger was in the pack too, but clearly not as dominant. As they were about 45 feet from her, Accalia, at half a year, couldn't run from the pack. Next to her, crawled Maheegan. Accalia gasped in shock as she appeared from nowhere.

"Don't startle me like that!" Accalia whispered.

Maheegan snorted. "Why?"

Accalia nodded her head towards the enemy pack, which Maheegan hadn't notice. They crouched down, and watched in horror as the enemy pack slowly made their way closer.

The pack was soon only about 20 feet away. Midnight shot her head in the air and smelled the air. She howled, and the pack joined in. Scar shot his hate-ridden eyes towards the bush where the pups lay. The pack began to trot towards the bush. Accalia couldn't run, but she couldn't bear to just stand there. She bolted out from the bushes, and tried to run away. Maheegan jumped after her, but she was grabbed by the tail by Scar.

"Your parents killed one of our own in a battle once! This is now our territory, and you are our first trespasser!" Midnight snarled.

Dagger quickly grabbed Accalia and dragger her over to the pack.

"Nobody trespasses on our territory!" He snarled.

As Scar gripped Maheegan's neck, Accalia reached over and gave him a face scratch, before being pulled away by Dagger. They cried desperately, but their pack couldn't hear them. Midnight picked Accalia up in her jaws. Suddenly, someone rammed into Midnight's side with her head. And another wolf gave Scar a deep wound in his hide. Accalia and Maheegan were out of the jaws of enemies, but they kept their eyes shut tight. All they heard were snarls that sounded more like roars.

"How dare you try to kill them! Innocent little pups!" Said a female voice.

I know that voice . . . Accalia thought.

"Nobody intrudes on our territory!" Said another familiar male voice.

Accalia gasped. Joy filled her heart. It was Nuntis and Fang!

The pups opened their eyes. Nuntis grabbed her sister, Midnight's back tightly. Fang had a hold of Dagger's neck, but Scar was on top of Fang, biting him hard. Fang got free, and Nuntis let go, they quickly dragged the pups to their feet and told them to run away. They pounced back on the enemy pack. As the pups stopped from a safe distance, they saw another wolf attacking Dagger. Somehow, some way, Fang and Nuntis' small pack chased the Midnight Howlers away. They howled happily, and a much 'fatter' Nuntis returned to the pups, with her pack behind her.

"You pups better be more careful. Stay in your pack territory." Nuntis smiled as the pups stared at her belly. "A lot has changed over winter. I will soon have pups of my own, hopefully not as troublesome as you girls!" She said, jokingly.

"Are you two alright?" Said the male stranger wolf.

They nodded.

"Oh, I almost forgot, this is Crimson. He's Nuntis' brother, and now a member of our pack." Said Fang.

They stared at the strong, brown wolf with specks of gray around his neck, and gray leg and tail. Crimson nudged the two girls, and walked off with Fang.

"You girls are right next to your territory; can you get home from here? I don't think your parents would be pleased to see me there." Nuntis asked.

"Yeah, we can." Accalia said. Nuntis nodded, and began to walk away. "Oh, and Nuntis!"

Nuntis turned around.

"Thanks." Accalia said with a grin.

"Anytime, ladies!" She said, and ran off after her pack.

Maheegan stared at the forest in shock of the entire thing.

"Accalia, you know when you scratched Scar?" She asked.

Accalia nodded.

"Were you trying to save me?" Maheegan asked.

"Of course, you are like a sister to me." Accalia replied.

"Thanks . . ." Maheegan said, quite shocked that her adoptive sister would try to save her after how mean she was to her.

They returned home, with quite the story to tell their pack.

Things were clearly heating up between the enemy packs.

Chapter Six

New Life

Three weeks later . . .

It was the end of another day for Nuntis' pack, now called the Silver Stream pack. Now, with three more members. Nuntis was nursing her babies, who were now two weeks old.

"Oh, Fang, darling! Come here, quick!" Fang rushed into the den.

"Is everything alright?" He said, as any new worried father would.

"Shh, yes, love. Look, the pups are beginning to open their eyes!" Nuntis said, looking lovingly at the largest pup opening his eyes.

"You remember the deal, then?" Fang said, his smile wide and his heart racing. "Time to begin naming them."

The sun was setting, and it grew darker in the den.

"You name the male; he is the first one to open his eyes all the way." Nuntis said, walking out of the den and looking at her pups inside.

Fang looked at the large male pup with a brown body, and black and grey markings.

"Alright, how about Arnou."

"Arnou. I like it." Nuntis said.

The second largest began to open his eyes; he was black with a grey tail and chest.

Crimson walked in.

"Oh my gosh!" He exclaimed as he looked at the pups opening their eyes.

"You name him." Nuntis said, looking at how excited Crimson was.

"R-really? Me? Um, ok. How about . . . Bullet?" Crimson said nervously.

"Very nice." Nuntis said.

It was now dark outside, and the littlest one, the female, opened her eyes. Her round eyes glowed in the darkness of the den.

"And of course, you name the last one." Fang said.

Nuntis looked at the grey pup with seemingly clear eyes, and splashes of light yellow.

"How about MoonEye, for her eyes are like the moon glowing in the dark." Nuntis said.

"Beautiful name." Fang said, and he howled in joy of the pup's milestone. The pack joined in.

The very first pups of the Silver Stream pack had a good chance of survival, bringing new life to the forest.

The next morning, Tikaani woke up early, and saw Ginny wondering off. He sneakily followed her from a good distance behind.

She made her way through Yellowstone as if it was a maze, going around territories and avoiding going through them. Ginny seemed to have the smarts of an adult wolf, she knew what dangers to stay away from, and what areas were safer. She finally stopped near a cliff. A tree was half fallen, giving her a 'stairway' up the cliff. Tikaani accidentally stepped on a twig, the snap made Ginny's head jolt in his direction, and she pounced on him without hesitation.

"Whoa!" He said as he was pinned.

"Oh, it's just you. What are you doing here?" She asked, stepping off him.

"Following you, of course! The question is, what are *you* doing here?" He asked.

"You know I go off and explore by myself. The best way to learn to survive, is to learn to survive alone." Ginny said, trotting up the steep fallen tree with ease.

"We are far too young to be so far away from the pack alone." Tikaani said, getting nervous.

"Maybe you, but I'm not! I may be as old as you, but I know my way around here better." She said, she lifted her head up, closed her eyes and continued to trot up the slanted tree.

"We should be getting back." He said, hearing distant howls. "We will be in so much trouble if we come back alone!"

"Oh alright!" She said, walking down the tree, and jumping off. "Come on, let's hurry!" She said, and they ran through the forest towards the pack territory.

They stopped at a river, and lapped up some of the rushing water. When they arrived home, their face filled with horror and shock as they saw a danger they would have never expected.

Chapter Seven

Nature, So Cruel

Ginny and Tikaani stood in shock as they arrived back home, only to find a grizzly bear on top of Convel, attacking him.

Tamaska pounced on the bear, biting his back hard, and the rest of the pack attacked, trying to get the large bear off their leader and father.

Finally, the bear ran off, tired of the pack attacking him. "Convel! Darling, are you alright?" Tamaska said, nudging her mate.

Convel groaned, and looks up at her.

"My side . . ." Convel groaned, he had a large, deep wound on his side.

"Oh, Convel . . ." Tamaska whined, licking his wounds.

"You'll be alright; I will take care of you." She said, as she laid her head on him.

Tamaska had also suffered large cuts across her back and shoulder, and they were both very weak. The rest of the pack suffered minor scratches, if any. All of the pups went running up to their leaders and parents, licking them and whining. It wasn't long before some hungry coyotes came along.

"Hmm, hmm . . . the pleasing smell of blood fills the air." Said the scratchy voice of the ragged coyote, smiling with his crooked yellow teeth.

"Back off!" Snarled Cuan, throwing his tail in the air and baring his teeth.

The coyote stepped back, and soon, several more came from the bushes. Cuan and Fluff had their paws full, chasing and charging at the annoying coyotes that kept coming back.

"I swear you lay one paw on our leaders and I will rip you to shreds!" Growled Fluff, as she bit a coyote's tail, before it scrambled away.

"Those cowardly coyotes won't dare come close to trying to eat a fully conscious wolf with a pack; I don't see why you even try so hard to chase them away." Said Olcan, the male beta wolf.

"Yeah, it's just pointless." Said Waya, the beta female.

Fluff growled at their sarcastic comments. Waya bit the back of Fluff's neck hard.

"Respect your higher ranks." She growled.

Fluff whined in pain. Cuan began to bear his teeth, and Olcan quickly put him in his place too. Waya gave Olcan a strange look, and they both let go, and walked over to the alpha pair.

"Feeling alright, Convel?" Olcan asked, with suspicion in his voice.

"Kind of . . . it hurts a lot." He said.

"Well, you two just get better." Waya said, and the two betas walked off.

"They are up to no good, I tell you!" Fluff whispered to Cuan.

"I know, but for now, we just have to keep wary." Cuan replied.

The pack spent the rest of the day at the den, as the alpha pair was too weak to go anywhere. Night came quickly, and the pack settled in.

Morning came, and the alpha pair woke a bit late, only to find that Waya and Olcan were dominating the poor pack members. Denny, who had moved down to the omega rank when Lilly died, even had scars from them. Tamaska and Convel were even weaker. Tamaska tried to get up, but couldn't.

"Olcan!" Waya said, making Olcan's head turn to her.

"I think it's time."

A crooked smile grew on their faces. Convel saw the blurry shapes of the beta pair trotting towards them. Olcan grasped the back of Convel's neck, and Waya did the same to Tamaska. They pressed their jaws harder until the alphas whined in submission.

"Well, look who's whining now . . ." Olcan said, as he pushed Convel down.

Waya stood over Tamaska.

"Only the strongest survive . . . and you're now a weakling." She said.

They walked away from the dominated alpha pair, or the ex-alpha pair now.

"Why you no-good sorry excuse for a wolf!" Cuan said, growling.

Olcan slashed Cuan's face, leaving two scratches across it. As Fluff seemed to try to make a move, Waya growled at her, and Fluff's tail dropped. The new alpha pair walked away from the harshly dominated pack, which was now under their command. Nevertheless, it was nature. Nature, so cruel.

Chapter Eight

A Change of Winds

"Come pack." Olcan ordered.

The pack whined and the pups licked the ex-alpha pair.

"I said come!" He ordered again.

Denny hung his head and tail and walked toward the new alphas, trying to avoid a beating. The other members whined a goodbye to their old alphas, and slowly walked to the pack. The alphas began walking, and the pack followed. However, the pups were still by the old alphas.

"Come with us, or stay back to die with your old leaders!" Waya snarled.

Accalia looked towards them, and looked back at her fellow pup-mates and parents with a heavy sigh.

"Pups . . . follow them. We are too weak to look after you. Go, we will take care of ourselves." Tamaska groaned.

Convel nudged them towards the pack. "Go." He said.

The pups slowly walked away, and went with the new pack, which were leaving the weak alphas behind.

The pack walked for a few minutes before stopping suddenly. A pack was in front of them, blocking them.

"This is our territory, get out." Said a female voice.

Accalia peeked around her pack, and she gasped. They ran into the Silver Stream pack! The new alpha pair stood their ground.

"Well we need to expand our territory. Go find another area for your puny pack." growled Olcan.

"Don't make us tell you again. Get out of our territory, now!" snarled Fang, raising his tail.

"Is that a challenge?" Olcan said, stepping forward, raising his tail.

The strong Crimson curled his lips back, baring his white teeth. Olcan, suddenly bit Fang's shoulder, and it turned into a fight. Waya jumped on Nuntis, biting her neck.

"Attack!" Waya told her pack. Fluff, Cuan, and Denny sat there. Crimson looked at them, expecting them to attack. Cuan bowed his head, showing that he wasn't going to attack. Crimson pounced on Waya, who had bitten Nuntis hard, and he pinned her. He threw Waya a few feet away. Olcan and Fang were viciously attacking each other, and Crimson joined in. Together, they pinned Olcan, biting him and baring teeth. He whined, having no other choice. Crimson stepped back, and Fang bit Olcan's paw hard.

"Never, ever, threaten my pack again, understand?" Fang said, snarling.

Olcan nodded, and Fang stepped off. Waya and Olcan ran behind the Windrush pack.

"Come pack." Olcan said, beginning to walk away.

"Come! NOW!" he snarled.

Fluff, surprisingly, jumped on him, and bit his neck so hard he gasped for breath.

"You and your little partner best run away while you have the chance. And if you EVER come into our lands again, well, you'll wish you hadn't . . ." Fluff said, snarling, and she backed off.

Olcan and Waya scampered off into the woods. Cuan's jaw was dropped in amazement.

"Where are Convel and Tamaska?" Nuntis asked.

"They were attacked by a bear; they survived before the beta pair took over. We must be getting back to them." Cuan said.

Nuntis and her pack nodded, and the Windrush pack took off back to their previous leaders.

They couldn't help but wonder if they were still alive.

When they arrived at the den, all was silent. Convel and Tamaska were gone, and a single coyote lick up the little puddle of blood they left.

Everyone stood in shock.

"What—where are Mom and Dad?" Caro, Maheegan's brother, asked.

"I—I don't know." Cuan said, hanging his head.

Denny chased the coyote away.

"They can't be dead, can they?" Denny said.

The pups looked at him in shock. Were their parents really dead? They didn't know. All they could do was hope.

Chapter Nine

The Leaders

The pack settled in, waiting, hoping, that the leaders would return. But there was no sign of them. The pack was only down to six half a year old pups, and three adults. The odds were certainly against them.

"Mahie . . ." Caro asked Maheegan.

"Do you think our parents are really . . . dead?" He said, hanging his head in sorrow.

"I really don't know, Caro. Our parents are strong, but they are injured and weak. We can only hope." She said with a gulp.

The next morning, the pack awoke, but there was still no sign of the leaders. Being as there were only three adults, one of which was a submissive omega, it seemed that Cuan and Fluff were in charge. Brownie and Caro play fought, while Tikaani still tried to make friends with Ginny. He stalked over to her, and sat next to her and the other girls, watching while Brownie played with Caro. Caro pinned Brownie and bit his ear. Accalia pounced on Caro from behind and pinned him.

"Ha-ha, rule of the hunter: expect the unexpected." She said, jumping off him, and trotting away.

Fluff howled, and the pups were soon back in order. They padded over the adults.

"Now pups-" Fluff began "You are young, nearly seven moons. But I think it is time you hunt."

"But we have already seen hunts." Maheegan added in a sarcastic voice.

"Yes, I know that. But you have never actually hunted, but that will change today." She said, smiling as the pups gasped in excitement.

"Come now," Cuan said. "Time to hunt."

Therefore, they made their way to the hunting grounds, where they saw a limping female deer.

"It is female, which means it has no antlers, and is very weak. I think you pups shall try and take it down on your own, with an adult nearby, of course." Fluff said, as the deer lay down.

Cuan looked at her as if she was crazy. Fluff ignored his look, and whispered to the pups.

"She lay down, now is a good time to attack. Go!" She said, and the pups charged off towards the doe.

Ginny pounced on her back and bit the back of the doe's neck. Accalia and Maheegan went in front of her, and bit the front and side of her neck. The males circled her, and bit around at her shoulders, side, and belly. The adults watched from a close distance. The doe tried to get up, but she stumbled and fell on her side. Soon, they killed her. The pups all howled in victory, and the adults joined in.

"If only our parents could have seen this!" Said Maheegan, digging into the carcass.

Little did they know, they were being watched.

The pack ate hungrily, and though the deer wasn't the best meal to sustain a pack, it held off their hunger. The pack finished, and began to walk off. The scent of strangers filled the air. They stopped, and Cuan growled.

"Who is there?" Out jumped a grey female loner, growling. "This is my territory! Get out with your pack, now!" She said.

A dark grey male walked out and stood next to her, and growled. Then, a third walked out. He was light brown, with a scar across his eye, and half a tail.

"Get out!" Snarled the dark grey male, who appeared to be the dominant male.

Cuan snarled. "Tiko . . . some things never change." Fluff looked at him strangely.

"Ah, brother . . . I see you have found yourself a little pack to protect." Tiko snarled.

"Now, get out of our territory!" Cuan snarled, and they slowly began to turn away.

"Peza . . ." Tiko whispered to the female.

The rest of what he whispered the pack couldn't hear. Suddenly, Peza jumped onto Fluff, biting her hard. Tiko tried to jump on Cuan, but he dodged, and pushed Peza off Fluff. Tiko and Cuan fought. Meanwhile, Peza pinned Fluff. She bit Fluff's neck, and didn't let go. Suddenly, another wolf pushed Peza off. She flew off and hit a tree, and went limp. The white rescuer was panting hard. A black wolf was snarling from the sidelines at Tiko. Finally, Tiko noticed his limp mate. He ran towards her, and the other male pack member stopped fighting, for he was alone, and ran off. When the fight calmed, the pups gasped. The rescuers were Tamaska and Convel! Their leaders had survived!

Peza got up, and she and Tiko ran off. The pups ran up to their leaders and licked them like crazy.

"So, how did you get rid of those mangy betas?" Convel asked.

"Well, they tried to fight the Silver Stream pack; little did they know we wouldn't help them!" Cuan laughed.

"I'm so glad you guys are alright!" Fluff said, going up to greet the leaders.

The pack headed home, and gave the leaders the TLC they needed. Tikaani headed into the den, lying down. Ginny walked in.

"Nice hunting today, I didn't think you had it in you." She said. Tikaani smiled.

The adults called her from outside.

"Coming! Duty calls." She said, winking at Tikaani.

She actually likes me! Tikaani thought.

And so, the pack slept that night, with high hopes and their leaders back.

Chapter Ten

Time Does Fly

Six months had passed since they found the leaders. The pups of the Windrush pack were now a year old, and the Silver Stream pack pups now six and a half months.

"Come on, Moon! We are going to the stream!" Arnou shouted at his sister.

"Sneaking out again?" MoonEye said with a smirk much like her father, Fang.

"We aren't stupid, we asked our parents!" Bullet growled.

"Hmmpf! Fine, I will go with you." she finally agreed, and followed her brothers to the stream.

Once they arrived, Arnou and Bullet play fought, while MoonEye tried to catch fish.

"Let me go!" Arnou growled when Bullet pinned him.

"Hah! Never!" Bullet said, as he stuck his chest out.

Arnou was caught by surprise when he no longer felt Bullet upon him. MoonEye grinned, as she turned the tables on Bullet.

"Never underestimate the power of a small wolf!" MoonEye said, and pounced off him.

Bullet snarled. "Then fight me!"

MoonEye began to growl, but a huge shadow grew over them.

"Uncle Crimson!" All the pups shouted.

"You pups aren't causing any trouble, now are you?" Crimson inquired.

"N-no, Uncle Crimson, just enjoying the stream." Bullet said, smiling innocently.

Crimson put his head down to Bullet's level.

"I know you better than that." He laughed. "Come, we have made a kill." He said, and the pups followed him to the carcass.

Only a few miles away, Accalia was alone, chewing on a hare she caught. She had been spending a lot of time away from the pack, even for a few nights at a time. She stopped eating when a scent of another wolf filled the area.

"Who is there?" She growled.

Out of the bushes came a muscular light grey wolf, about a year and a half.

"What is a pretty wolf like you doing alone?" He said.

"Answer my question, who are you?" She snarled.

"Gorg. I'm a loner. Now you answer mine." He replied.

Accalia took a deep breath and raised her head high. "I'm not alone."

"I don't see a pack." Gorg insisted.

"What are you doing here?" Accalia said, beginning to bare her fangs, Gorg was in Windrush territory.

"Ah, just searching for a mate." He said, swishing his tail.

"Well, you're not going to find that here, now are you?" Said Brownie, stepping out of the bushes behind Accalia.

"Is that a challenge?" Gorg growled, raising his tail.

"You're in our territory, leave now!" Brownie snarled.

Gorg walked to Accalia and nuzzled her; she pulled away, and went behind Brownie. Gorg slashed Brownie's eye, leaving a bloody scratch. Brownie swiftly bit his muzzle, until he whimpered. Brownie let go, and Gorg ran off.

"Oh, Brownie, that looks so painful!" Accalia said, licking his wound.

"I'm alright," He said, lying down.

Accalia lay down beside him, and nuzzled him. They slept for the night underneath the tree, unaware what was to come.

The next morning, Accalia and Brownie returned to their pack, after hearing howls from the leaders.

"I'm glad your back." Tamaska said coolly as she bumped heads with Accalia and Brownie.

"You're spending an awful lot of time away from the pack, dear. I know you are still young, but please don't make the mistake I did, and tell me when you wish to disperse. Otherwise, I will be worried day and night about where you went!" Tamaska laughed.

Just then, a howl of pain echoed across the area. The pack's ears shot up.

"Convel, where is Caro?" Tamaska said in a worried, serious voice. Convel looked horrified.

"*No.*" he whispered, running off in the direction of the yell, with Tamaska and the pack close behind.

"Caro!" Maheegan yelled as she saw her brother laying there, in the rocky bottom of the small waterfall, limp.

He was bleeding from his neck, which lay in an awkward position, it appeared broken. Tamaska jumped into the somewhat shallow water, and nudged her son repeatedly, along with Convel. The pups ran over to him, and licked their brother. Caro, the pure black male that grew up with the pups, didn't wake. The pack let out mournful howls and cries of sadness. They could hardly believe it.

"Lilly, my sister," Tamaska said quietly looking at the sky, "Watch over my Caro, please . . ." she said, hanging her head in sadness.

Convel turned away, for he couldn't bear to look at his son any longer.

"Come on, let's go." He said, comforting Tamaska as she walked up next to him.

The pack followed the leader's home.

Chapter Eleven

Decisions

A week passed, it was now the beginning of winter. At the Silver Stream territory, the pups were awakening.

"It's so cold . . ." Arnou said, walking out of the den.

"Ooh! What's that?" MoonEye exclaimed as a snowflake fell from the sky above her.

She trotted beneath it, and shivered as it melted on her muzzle.

"Look, there is more!" Arnou said as more snow began to fall.

"What's all this?" Bullet said, stretching.

"It's called snow. It falls during winter." Crimson said from behind them.

The pups looked up at the sky in amazement, and had a good time playing in the fresh snow.

In the Windrush territory, Ginny was walking alone.

"Eep!" she yelped as she was pinned to the ground by Dagger.

She immediately snarled. He bit her leg, causing her to yelp loudly.

"Get off her!" growled a voice.

Ginny looked up, but her vision was blurry, and she couldn't quite make out the grey male.

"Ha! Or you'll what, tiny?" Dagger shrugged.

The male jumped on Dagger, knocking him off Ginny. She jumped up, and helped attack him. Being outnumbered, Dagger scampered off into the forest. Ginny looked over to see the male was Tikaani.

"You—saved me . . ." Ginny stammered.

"Well, you are worth saving." Tikaani replied.

"Thanks." Ginny said, blushing.

"Come on, let's go home." Tikaani said, beginning to walk away.

"Actually, Tikaani . . ." she said, sighing heavy. "I'm going to disperse."

"Disperse? So soon?" He whined and lowered his head.

"Yes, and Accalia probably will soon, too. I know it is hard for you, Tikaani. But we are adults now, and we have to make our own decisions. And I have made mine. I am sorry . . . Goodbye, Tikaani." she said, licking his muzzle, and running off.

"Goodbye, Ginny." he whispered, watching her run into the forest.

On his way home, he ran into Accalia.

"Hey Tik, what's up?" Accalia chirped.

"Ginny . . . she is gone. She dispersed." he said, glancing up at his sister.

Accalia knew this, but she felt horrible for her brother. She gazed into his sad eyes, and she knew he was heartbroken.

Just then, a strange female ran through the heavy forest Accalia and Tikaani were in. She stopped, skidding dirt on Accalia's white pelt.

The female was a white one, about three years, with familiar dark markings.

"Who are you, stranger?" growled Accalia.

"I swear I'm no threat! Let me pass in peace! Dare you fight me; you'll be the one in danger!" The stranger growled.

"She meant your name." Tikaani said sarcastically.

"Kiyiya! I haven't had a pack since I had my pups a year ago!"

"MOM?" Accalia gasped.

"Accalia? Tikaani? Is it really you? Oh my gosh! My pups!"

The pups ran up to her and licked her like crazy.

"How did you two ever survive?" she asked.

"Well—the Windrush pack adopted us!" Accalia said, licking her mother.

"Is that so? Well . . . I guess my sister does have a soft spot for pups." She scoffed.

"Sister?" the pups said in unison.

"Yes, Tamaska is your aunt." She confirmed.

"Well, come on, mom. Come meet the pack." Tikaani said, nodding towards the direction of the den.

"Err . . . darlings; I don't think they will accept me." Kiyiya said in a small voice.

"Well, they are nice! It is worth a try, come on!" Accalia said, running up beside her brother.

They walked to the den, unsure whether or not the leaders would accept Kiyiya.

As they arrived, Kiyiya stayed in the bushes while Accalia and Tikaani walked up to the leaders.

"We found something. Something, which I hope you accept." Accalia said, smiling sweetly, nuzzling her aunt and uncle.

"We found . . . our mother." Gasps and exclaims came from the pack members, but the alpha pair stayed silent.

"Really? Where is she?" Tamaska said, scanning the area.

Kiyiya stepped from the bushes, her tail down and ears back.

"Hello, Tamaska. I want to thank you. Without you, my pups would never have survived."

"Well, I couldn't just leave them there to starve." she said, walking up to Kiyiya.

Seeing as the adults were getting nowhere fast, Accalia stepped in.

"So . . . can she join the pack? Please . . . ?" she said, whining.

After long moments of silence, Tamaska replied, "If your mother wishes to stay, she is welcome into the pack."

The pups, which were nearly fully grown, were thrilled. However, Tikaani's happiness was short-lived, as he remembered his dear friend, Ginny.

Would he ever see her again?

Chapter Twelve

The Difficulties of Growing Up

Seven months later . . .

Accalia stretched in the morning sun, her claws digging into the earth. She was now a year and nine months old . . . and a dispersal. Though most wolves prefer to disperse around two years, Accalia dispersed early. She found it harder to survive alone than she ever thought. *Poor Ginny . . . I wonder if she knew how dangerous it was. She was so young to disperse.* Accalia thought. *Maybe she'll find a mate. Or when Tikaani disperses, they could find each other.* She shook her head, and went out to find some food that morning. It was fall, but there was an unusual shortage of food, if the shortage got worse, it might be Accalia's first famine. After an hour of searching, she found a fat hare, which she stalked.

She was just about to pounce when something startled the hare, and it bolted in the opposite direction. Accalia gave chase, but she couldn't seem to keep up. She stopped suddenly, her heart beating wildly. Something from the bushes had snatched the hare. Accalia took a few steps back nervously. Out of the bushes walked a brown female, with tints of gold. Seeing how strong the female looked, Accalia quickly sped backwards. The female seemed to chuckle at this, and began to eat the hare. Accalia began to walk away; there was no way she would get this meal from the female.

"Chin up, kid. Next time, Bronze probably won't be there to steal your food." Accalia shot her glance around to the female, apparently named Bronze.

She snorted and continued her walk away. After a few minutes of walking, she heard a howl echo from a few miles away. Was it her old family, or an enemy pack? She didn't know, and whatever it was, she didn't want to find out. She bolted in the opposing direction, toward Amethyst Mountain.

When she arrived, she lay down in a grassy hillside, overlooking Yellowstone.

"I wonder what my family is doing now." She asked herself with a sigh.

A growl came from behind her. Before she had a moment to move, she was knocked over and pinned.

"Be still, trespasser! What are you doing here?" Growled the brown male on top of her.

Accalia couldn't move, she thought she was certainly a goner.

"Nothing!" She said, looking away from the male.

She glanced at him, and realized how familiar he looked.

"Brownie . . . is that you?" Accalia asked.

"Accalia? Oh, it is so good to see you!" He said, licking her chin.

"Yeah, it is. Brownie?"

"Yeah?" Brownie replied.

"Uh . . . can you get off me now?" Accalia said, still pinned.

"Oh, yeah sorry . . ." He said, stepping off her.

"So, it's pretty hard to find food now-a-days, huh?" She said, remembering the morning.

"Oh, that reminds me, come here! I found a carcass!" He said, running in the direction of the forest.

She laughed and ran after him, maybe she did stand a better chance of survival that Fall, after all.

* * *

Meanwhile, in Silver Stream territory . . .

"Shh, stalk quietly, stay calm, and get ready. And always have a strategy." Fang whispered to his pups, who were learning how to hunt.

"Good, now Arnou, you and Bullet go on each side of the elk. Brother . . ." Nuntis said looking at Crimson.

"You will go for the front of the neck, and MoonEye—you will try to pounce on it, and bite the back of her neck. Fang and I will be chasing in the back, but the important thing is that you pups do most of the work." She finished, and looked towards the female elk.

"Get ready . . . And . . . GO!" she shouted, and they gave chase.

Crimson raced ahead of the pups, and was soon beside the elk. The pups caught up, and soon everyone was in position. They snapped and pounced at the elk, wounding its sides badly. When Crimson got a hold of her neck, the elk stopped, trying to kick him off. But it was no use. They took the elk down quickly.

"Great job, pack!" Nuntis howled, as they dug into the carcass.

Chapter Thirteen

The Ultimate Sacrifice

When the Silver Stream pack arrived back at the den, they found their territory was filled with the scent of a rival pack. Not just any rival pack—but the Midnight Howlers.

"Scent is about an hour old, I would guess they are gone by now." Crimson said, trying to comfort the pups. But little did they know what horror was happening on the other side of the territory.

Just three miles away . . .

"Let me go, you bloody fools!" Growled a beautiful white wolf, pinned by Midnight and her pack.

"Why should we? You came into *our* lands, you are a trespasser!" Midnight snarled. "Who are you, and what business do you have here?"

"I am Adelita, and I didn't realize these were *your* lands!" she said, almost mockingly.

"Humph. Well . . ." chuckled Midnight. "You won't make that mistake again, now will you? Finish her!"

Scar bit her neck harshly, and Adelita let out a cry of pain that echoed throughout.

"Who do you think that is?" Accalia questioned.

Before Brownie could answer, Bronze stepped out from the bushes.

"Adelita!" She said, running in the direction of the noise. Accalia and Brownie exchanged looks of confusion. Accalia followed her without hesitation, leaving Brownie a bit confused; but he followed, too. Bronze jumped on Scar, knocking him down. Accalia stopped, and watched from the sides. The Midnight Howlers pack had grown quite a bit since she last saw them.

"Well, well, well . . . if it isn't my pathetic sister . . . ." Midnight chuckled, staring at Bronze coldly.